SUPER TURBO

AND THE FOUNTAIN OF DOOM

By Lee Kirby
Illustrated by George O'Connor

LITTLE SIMON

New York London Toronto Sydney New Delhi

This book is a work of fiction. Any references to historical events, real people, or real places are used fictitiously. Other names, characters, places, and events are products of the author's imagination, and any resemblance to actual events or places or persons, living or dead, is entirely coincidental.

LITTLE SIMON

An imprint of Simon & Schuster Children's Publishing Division

1230 Avenue of the Americas, New York, New York 10020

First Little Simon paperback edition August 2019. Copyright © 2019 by Simon & Schuster, Inc. All rights reserved, including the right of reproduction in whole or in part in any form. LITTLE SIMON is a registered trademark of Simon & Schuster, Inc., and associated colophon is a trademark of Simon & Schuster, Inc. For information about special discounts for bulk purchases, please contact Simon & Schuster Special Sales at 1-866-506-1949 or business@simonandschuster.com. The Simon & Schuster Speakers Bureau can bring authors to your live event. For more information or to book an event contact the Simon & Schuster Speakers Bureau at 1-866-248-3049 or visit our website at www.simonspeakers.com. Designed by Jay Colvin. The text of this book was set in Little Simon Gazette.

Manufactured in the United States of America 0719 MTN 10 9 8 7 6 5 4 3 2 1

Cataloging-in-Publication Data for this title is available from the Library of Congress.

ISBN 978-1-5344-4507-9 (hc)

ISBN 978-1-5344-4506-2 (pbk)

ISBN 978-1-5344-4508-6 (eBook)

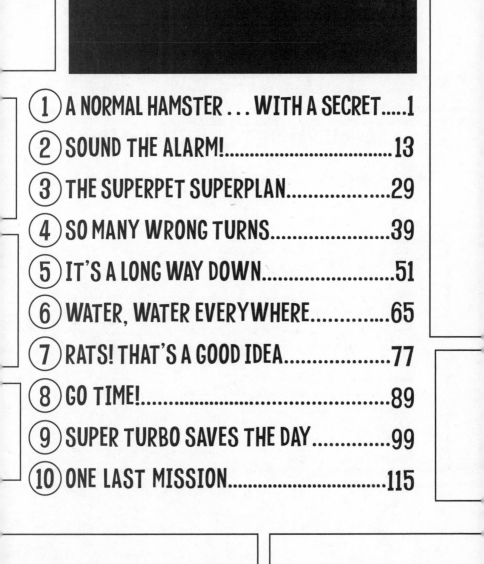

A NORMAL HAMSTER ... WITH A SECRET

BEHOLD! SUNNYVIEW ELEMENTARY SCHOOL! INSIDE THESE WALLS THERE IS A BIG SECRET.

There's the secret right now, just sitting there in Classroom C. No, not that second-grade student. Behind him, in the hamster cage. What's that you say? A hamster cage is a strange place to find a secret? Not if the secret is, in fact, a hamster!

Turbo the hamster leaned back

in his comfy cage, his arms crossed behind his head. One tiny hamster foot rested on the opposite tiny hamster knee. He whistled to himself, daydreaming about what a very lucky hamster he was. He had his own cage, all the food and water he could ever want, lots of fans, and a whole classroom to protect. That's right: *protect*.

You see, the secret is that Turbo is no ordinary hamster. He is *secretly* the amazing, the incredible, the stupendous SUPER TURBO!

Suddenly Turbo got a strange tickly feeling up the back of his neck.

Finally, the bell rang. School was out for the day! The kids of Classroom C grabbed their coats and books and left the room.

Whew! thought Turbo. *Pretending to be non-super is more work than actually being super!* He went over to his water bottle to grab a drink.

Well, he *tried* to grab a drink. Nothing was coming out of the water bottle. Because it was empty!

Turbo had to act fast. Ms. Beasley, the second-grade teacher, was just getting ready to leave. If she went home, Turbo wouldn't have any water until the next morning!

Turbo started squeaking, trying to

get Ms. Beasley's attention. "Yes, yes, good night, Turbo," the teacher called out, closing the door. "I'll see you tomorrow."

Squeak! Squeak! Squeak! squeaked Turbo, hopping up and down and waving his little hamster paws in the air. But it was too late. The light turned off, the door shut, and Ms. Beasley was gone.

What was Turbo going to do now?

SOUND THE ALARM!

Turbo licked his dry lips. He was really thirsty. Like, really, *really* thirsty.

"I shouldn't have run on my wheel so much when I was trying to act like a normal hamster," he said aloud to no one in particular.

Turbo had to get water, and fast.

Now, if he *were* just a normal hamster, he might be out of luck. But, remember, Turbo isn't a normal hamster.

Turbo shimmied up the side of
his cage and popped off the top.
He leapt from his cage onto the

bookcase, executing a perfect superhero landing.

Then he climbed
down from the
bookcase. He ran
over to the vent
that connected
Classroom C to all
of the other class-
rooms in Sunny-
view Elementary.
The superpets used
the vents as their
own personal high-
way, and also as a way
to call emergency super-
pet meetings to order.

What's that? You thought Super Turbo was the only superhero pet in Sunnyview Elementary? No way! There's a whole league of super-pet superheroes! It's called . . . the Superpet Superhero League.

Super Turbo picked up a metal ruler. If he banged the vent one time with the ruler, it meant: *All's well.*

Well, everything certainly isn't all well, thought Super Turbo.

If he banged the vent two times with the ruler, it meant: *Hey, I'm hungry. Who wants to go to the cafeteria?*

Super Turbo thought about this for a second. It was close, but he was thirsty, not hungry. And he didn't particularly want to go to the cafeteria.

If Super Turbo banged three times with the ruler, it meant: *Emergency, come quick!*

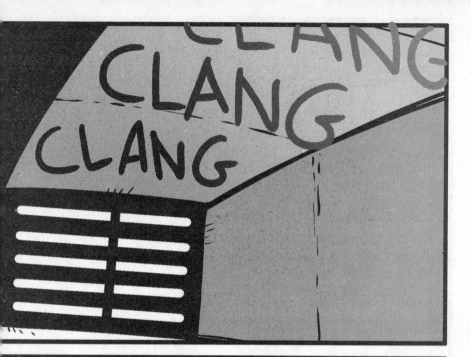

CLASSROOM A:
LEO, AKA THE GREAT GECKO! THE SUPERPETS'
SUPER LEADER! CAN STICK TO WALLS!

In almost no time flat, the super-pets arrived in Classroom C.

"What's going on, Super Turbo?" asked the Great Gecko, concerned. "Is there trouble?"

"Is it that rat Whiskerface and his no-good Rat Pack?" asked Wonder Pig, cracking her knuckles.

"It's not another evil pencil sharpener, is it?" said the Green Winger.

"No, no, it's nothing like that," said Super Turbo, slightly embarrassed. "I'm all out of water."

"No water, huh?" said Boss Bunny, paws on his utility belt.

"I'd offer you some of mine," said

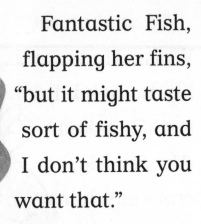

Fantastic Fish, flapping her fins, "but it might taste sort of fishy, and I don't think you want that."

Super Turbo had to agree. He loved Fantastic Fish, but he didn't want to drink the water she was swimming in.

"Well, what should we do?" asked Captain Chameleon. "Where can we get Super Turbo a drink?"

"IIIII KNOOOW."

The superpets all whirled to face
the vent. A spooky voice echoed
from the darkness.

"I KNOW JUST THE PLACE!"

THE SUPERPET SUPERPLAN

The superpets all stared at the vent where the spooky voice had come from.

Boss Bunny jumped into Wonder Pig's arms. "Is it a g-ghost?" he asked, teeth chattering.

The spooky voice continued from the darkness. "WE CAN GET . . .

SUPER TURBO . . . A DRINK"—
suddenly Professor Turtle stepped
into view—"at the water fountain . . .
in the hallway."

"Professor Turtle!" exclaimed
Super Turbo, letting out a sigh.

"Sorry, I forgot to mention," said
Captain Chameleon, turning a
shade of pink, "when we heard the
signal, I ran ahead of Professor
Turtle to see what was so urgent."

Professor Turtle smiled. "I'm . . .
not . . . exactly . . . the . . . fastest . . .
runner."

"The water fountain, though?"
asked the Green Winger. "Why don't
we just get Super Turbo a drink at
one of our cages? Wouldn't
that be easier?"

"Half of the fun of
being a superpet is
doing things school
kids and teachers
will never know
about!" said the Great
Gecko. "The other half

is saving the school from evil, of course," he added.

"I *have* always wanted to drink from the water fountain," said Super Turbo. His mouth was getting really dry now.

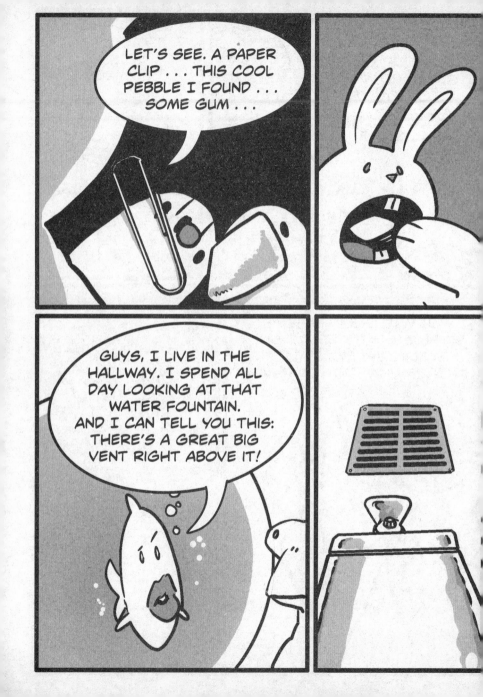

The superpets
flew into action. The
Great Gecko thought it would be a
good idea if a couple of superpets
stayed behind to keep an eye out for
evil. Fantastic Fish and Professor

Turtle volunteered, since there was no way they were going to be able to get up and onto the water fountain anyway.

The rest of the superpets climbed into the vent.

"Okay, Wonder Pig!" yelled the Great Gecko. "Lead the way to adventure!"

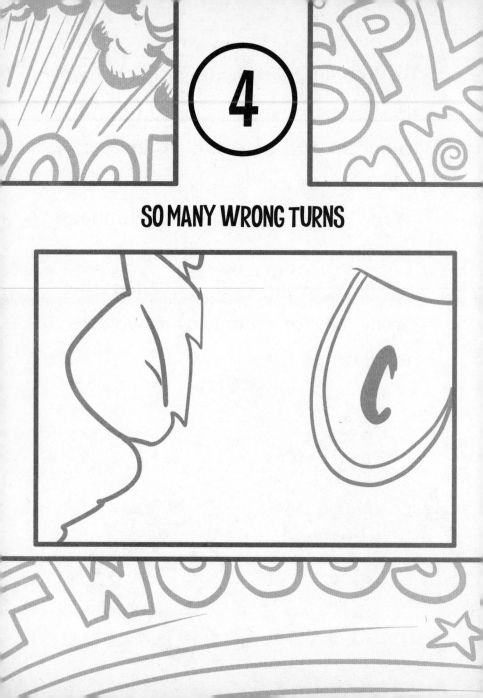

4

SO MANY WRONG TURNS

"This doesn't look like adventure.
This looks like . . . the janitor's
closet."

Super Turbo, the Great Gecko,
Wonder Pig, the Green Winger,
Boss Bunny, and Captain Chameleon stood looking down from the
open vent Wonder Pig had led them

to. All they could see were mops, buckets, and bottles of cleaning fluid.

"Hm . . . ," said Wonder Pig, thoughtfully rubbing her chin. "Yeah, this is definitely the janitor's closet."

"What happened?" asked Super Turbo. "You're normally so good at directions."

"Well, I've never had any reason to go to the water fountain before," Wonder Pig said, shrugging.

The superpets went back into the vent system.

THEY WENT THIS WAY.

AND THAT WAY.

OVER HERE.

THROUGH THAT.

UNTIL . . .

"Are we . . . outside?" asked Captain Chameleon, blinking.

"We sure are!" said the Green Winger. "Hey, isn't that the tree that Nutkin and her Flying Ninja Squirrels live in?"

"I think so!" said the Great Gecko.

"Should we wave to them?" asked Wonder Pig.

"Good idea!" said the Great Gecko. The superpets spent the next few minutes waving at the tree.

"Guys, I'm getting really thirsty," said Super Turbo.

"Sorry, Super Turbo," said Wonder Pig, heading back into the vent. "I think I know the way now."

THEY WENT UP HERE.

DOWN THERE.

WHAT IS THAT?

AROUND THIS.

"Oh man!" said Wonder Pig, hitting her forehead. "We're outside again."

"*Pee-yew!*" said Boss Bunny, holding his nose. "It stinks!"

"It sure does!" said the Green Winger, covering her beak. "And look, that's why! This is where they keep the garbage!"

"And that's not all!" cried Super Turbo, pointing. "There's Whisker-face and his Rat Pack!"

"Hey, you rats!" the Great Gecko yelled down from the vent. "What are you doing?"

Whiskerface and the Rat Pack looked up at the superpets.

"We're going through the garbage!" yelled Whiskerface. "A rat's
gotta eat! What are you guys doing?"

"Uh, we're on patrol," stammered
the Great Gecko. "Yeah, that's it. So,
uh, just you rats watch out!

"Sorry about this, guys," said Wonder Pig. "I definitely know the right path now."

The superpets took a few more twists and turns until, finally, they came upon another vent exit. Wonder Pig and Captain Chameleon popped it open. The superpets all looked down. About three feet below them was the water fountain.

"Behold!" said the Great Gecko, throwing his arms wide. "We made it!"

5

IT'S A LONG WAY DOWN

Wonder Pig let out a whistle. "That's a pretty long way down. I think maybe I should wait up here, and uh, keep an eye out for evil."

The superpets had been perched on the ledge, looking at the water fountain down below, for about five minutes now. They were so close, and yet so far.

"Let me think about this," said Boss Bunny. He pulled out the cool pebble he had found from his utility belt and dropped it over the edge. It took a surprisingly long time before the super-pets heard it hit the ground below.

"Yeah, I'm definitely waiting up here," said Wonder Pig.

"Maybe I should just try to wait until tomorrow for water," said Super Turbo uncertainly.

"Guys! Guys!" exclaimed the Great Gecko. "We can't quit now, not when we're so close! We can do this!"

WELL, I CAN JUST FLY OVER. BUT I'M NOT SURE I CAN CARRY EITHER OF YOU THAT FAR.

I'M A BUNNY. I CAN HOP!

Now it was just Super Turbo and Wonder Pig. As unimpressive as Boss Bunny's leap had been, he made it way farther than Super Turbo would be able to. How was he going to get there?

"Come on, Super Turbo, you can do it!" called the superpets from down below.

Can I? thought Super Turbo to himself. Then he had an idea. He whispered something in Wonder Pig's ear.

"That's totally crazy," she said with a smile. "I love it."

"Hey, guys!" Super Turbo yelled down. "I need you to turn on the water fountain and fill up the bowl!"

"Is he going to do what I think he is?" the Great Gecko asked Captain Chameleon.

"I think so!" she replied.

The Great Gecko and Captain Chameleon turned the knob on the water fountain. Water, beautiful water started spilling out of the bubbler. Up above, Super Turbo licked his lips. Boss Bunny stuck a chewed-up piece of gum into the drain of the fountain.

Soon enough, the bowl looked like a tiny swimming pool. Or, to any small animal, a regular-size swimming pool.

HE'S DOING IT!

ACK!

The superpets all cheered. That was the coolest thing they had seen in a long time.

"That was just incredible, Super Turbo!" said the Great Gecko.

"Wow! Amazing!" added Captain Chameleon.

"You were really flying, Super Turbo!" said the Green Winger.

"Eh, I could've done that," said Boss Bunny.

But Super Turbo didn't say anything back to any of them. He was too busy drinking that sweet, sweet water.

6

WATER, WATER EVERYWHERE

After Super Turbo was done drinking, he, Boss Bunny, the Great Gecko,
Captain Chameleon, and the Green
Winger splashed around in the
water fountain. They floated on
their backs, they swam laps, and
Boss Bunny performed some sort of
weird water show.

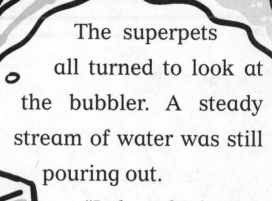

The superpets all turned to look at the bubbler. A steady stream of water was still pouring out.

"I thought it was getting pretty deep in here," said Captain Chameleon.

"Hmm," said Super Turbo. "I thought the water fountain was supposed to turn off by itself."

"Me too," said the Great Gecko, leaping onto the knob of the water fountain. He pulled it back and forth several times. "Oh no. I think we turned it too far. I think it's broken!"

"Hey, guys!" Wonder Pig yelled from above. "Take a look!"

The superpets rushed to the edge of the bowl to see where she was pointing. They looked down. The water was now overflowing, and a puddle had started to form on the floor below.

"Oh no!" yelled the Great Gecko.
"We're going to flood the whole
school! This is not the adventure I
imagined!"

Super Turbo knew they had to
act fast. "If we can't stop the water,
maybe we can unplug the drain?
Boss Bunny, can you pull out your
gum?"

Boss Bunny dove into the water.

Only his bunny feet were
visible now. After a few
seconds, he came up. "It's
no good!" he said, spit-
ting out water. "The gum's

been sucked too far into the drain. I can't get it out!"

The water was spilling over the side of the fountain like a waterfall now. The puddle had gotten so big it was beginning to seep under the doors of nearby classrooms.

"I'll go to the janitor's closet to get sponges and mops!" Wonder Pig announced. "Now that I've been there once, I know how to get back."

She disappeared into the vents.

"I'll go get Fantastic Fish and Professor Turtle," said the Green Winger, taking flight. "I have a feeling we're going to need all the superpets for this one."

"In the meantime, we have to see if there's anything we can do here," said Super Turbo.

HOW WILL WE STOP IT? WE ALREADY KNOW THE KNOB IS BROKEN!

MAYBE WE COULD USE SOMETHING TO BLOCK THE WATER? BOSS BUNNY, DO YOU HAVE ANYTHING ON YOUR BELT THAT WOULD WORK?

NO, I USED THE GUM ALREADY . . .

BUT I KNOW WHAT I MUST DO!

BLUB GLUB BLUB

BOSS BUNNY, NO! YOU CAN'T DRINK IT ALL!

THAT BRAVE FOOL!

Captain Chameleon, Super Turbo, and the Great Gecko ran to look over the side. To their relief, Boss Bunny was fine. What was not fine was that he was now practically swimming in the water down below.

"Now what?" Super Turbo asked the others.

7

RATS! THAT'S A GOOD IDEA

The superpets who were still at the fountain decided they couldn't just wait up there. They had to get down.

Soon after they got to the ground, Wonder Pig returned from the janitor's closet with a bunch of sponges. The superpets were now making a kind of dam with them, but it was a

big, soggy, mushy dam. It held back
some of the water, but not enough.
Fantastic Fish was using her Fish
Tank like a bull-
dozer, pushing
the heavy,
soggy
sponges

into place. "A few more inches of water and I won't even need my Fish Tank to get around!" she said, joking. None of the other superpets laughed.

This all started because I selfishly wanted a drink! thought Super Turbo.

As a superpet, it was his job to protect Sunnyview Elementary! Now he was worried that, because of his actions, Sunnyview Elementary might end up completely underwater! And after that, maybe the whole world would!

Super Turbo was suddenly snapped out of his thoughts by a squeaking voice. "What are you superpests doing?!"

The superpets all stopped what they were doing to face . . .

"Whiskerface!" yelled the Great Gecko. "Wouldn't you like to know?"

"Well, yeah, I

would," said Whiskerface. "Are you stuporpets trying to flood the school?!"

"Well, we weren't *trying* to," Boss Bunny said quietly to himself.

"Obviously we're trying to *save* the school from a flood!" said the Great Gecko, scoffing.

"The water fountain won't turn off!" yelled Captain Chameleon.

"And the drain's clogged!" cried the Green Winger.

"And there doesn't seem to be an off switch!" added Fantastic Fish.

OH YES . . . IT HAS CONTROLS . . . FOR THE HEAT . . . THE AIR-CONDITIONING . . . AND THE WATER!

THERE'S AN OFF SWITCH? WHY DIDN'T YOU SAY SOMETHING EARLIER?

HEY . . . I JUST . . . GOT HERE!

"Eek! Water! I hate water!" Whiskerface squeaked and jumped back as a drop of water touched his foot. "I'm getting out of here before the whole hallway floods!"

He shook his little rat fist at the superpets. "I don't know what you guys did, but you better fix this!" And with that, Whiskerface disappeared into a hole in the wall.

The superpets all looked at each other. Whiskerface was right. It was up to them to fix this flood!

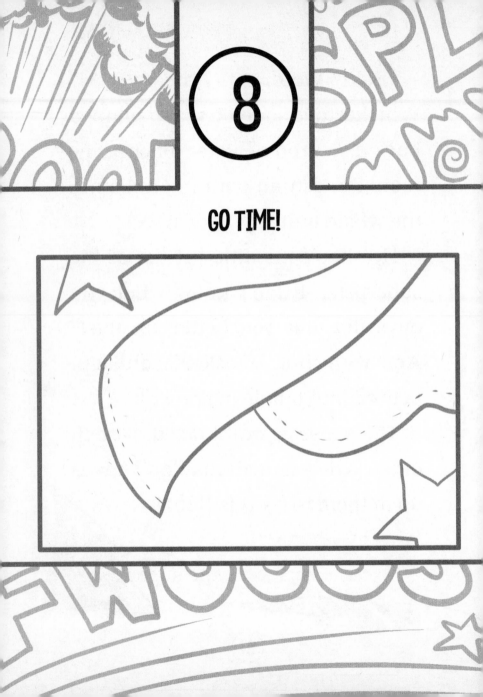

8

GO TIME!

Super Turbo turned to the rest of the superpets. "Okay, team. It's go time. We better split up our forces. Half of us will stay here to hold back the flood. The other half will go to the basement to turn off the water. Who's with me?"

"We are!" cried all the superpets.

"Excellent!" said the Great Gecko. "Super Turbo, you can be in charge of the Boiler Room Mission! I'll stay here and help stop this flood from spreading!"

AND I'LL GO TOO. YOU GUYS MIGHT NEED SOME MUSCLE DOWN THERE. BESIDES, I KNOW THE WAY.

COUNT ME IN! I'VE ALWAYS WANTED TO SEE THE BASEMENT.

AND I'LL . . . COME ALONG . . .

"You're sure you know the way, Wonder Pig?" asked Super Turbo, running beside her in the vents.

"Oh yeah, for sure!" said Wonder Pig. "Because I know that we just need to find a vent that points down! In fact, here's one now."

Wonder Pig stood in front of a deep, dark hole that stretched down into . . . well, the boiler room, Super Turbo guessed. Though all he could see was darkness.

"D-down there?" he asked.

Wonder Pig nodded. "Yeah, this should take us right to the boiler room. We just jump into it and zip down like it's a giant slide."

"But what if there's nothing to stop us at the end and we just slide . . . into the boiler?!" Super Turbo said, his teeth now chattering slightly.

"I'll go down first," offered the Green Winger. "That way, if it's open on the other end, I can just fly out."

The superpets agreed that was a good idea.

The Green Winger dove into the chute. A few minutes went by. Super Turbo was starting to get a

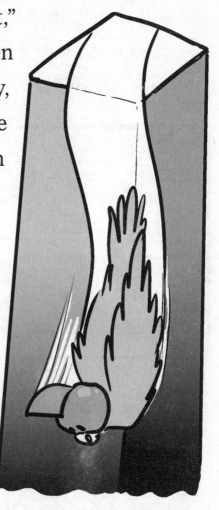

little nervous. Finally, they heard the Green Winger's voice. She sounded very far away.

"Well you heard her!" said Wonder Pig. "Last one in is a rotten egg!"
Wonder Pig jumped down the hole. Captain Chameleon glanced

at Super Turbo, shrugged, and then she too jumped in. Super Turbo was the only one left now.

"Well," he said with a gulp. "I guess I'm the rotten egg." And then he jumped down the hole.

9

SUPER TURBO SAVES THE DAY

Super Turbo couldn't see anything, but he could tell he was sliding fast—*very* fast.

HE SLID THIS WAY.

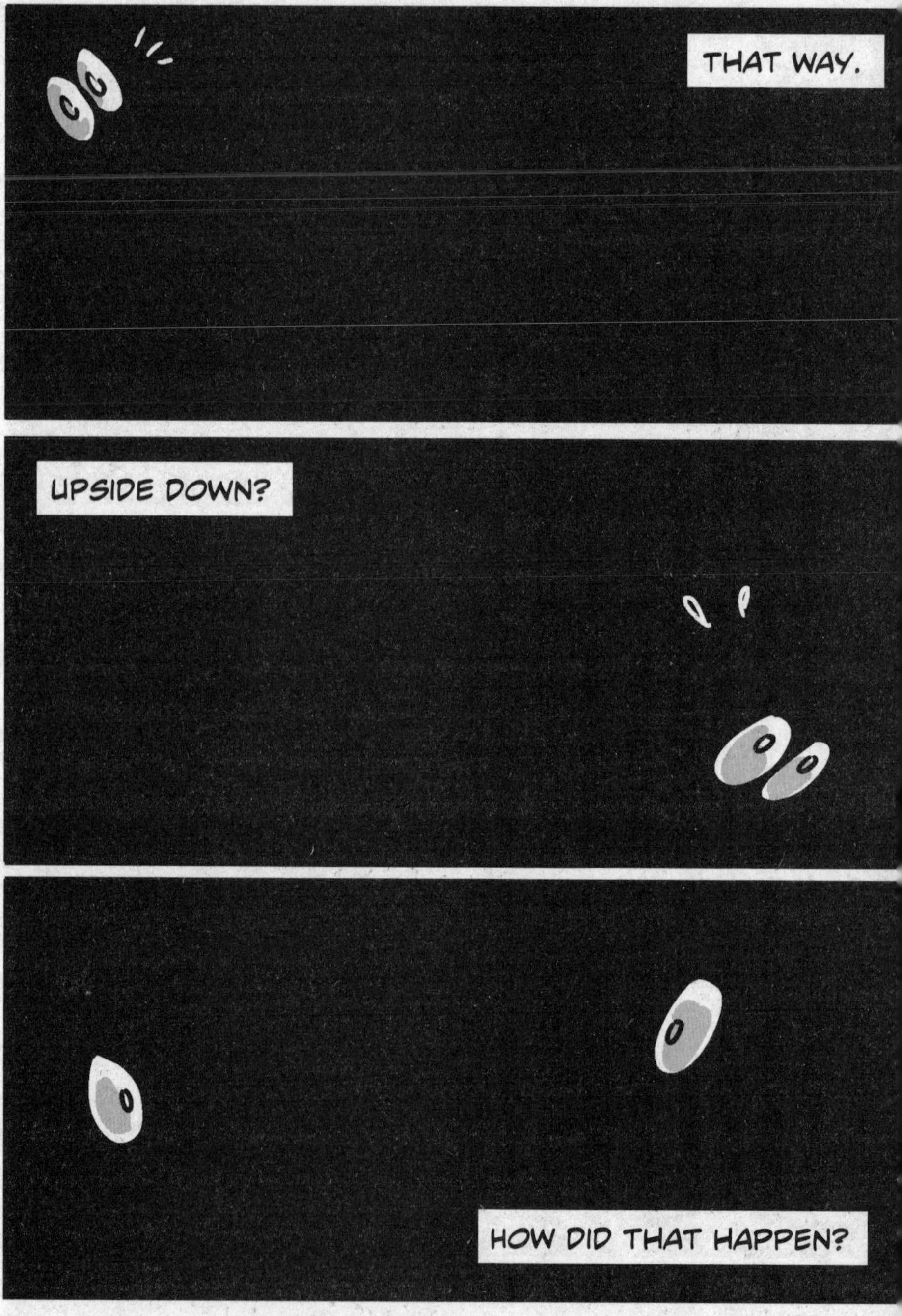
THAT WAY.
UPSIDE DOWN?
HOW DID THAT HAPPEN?

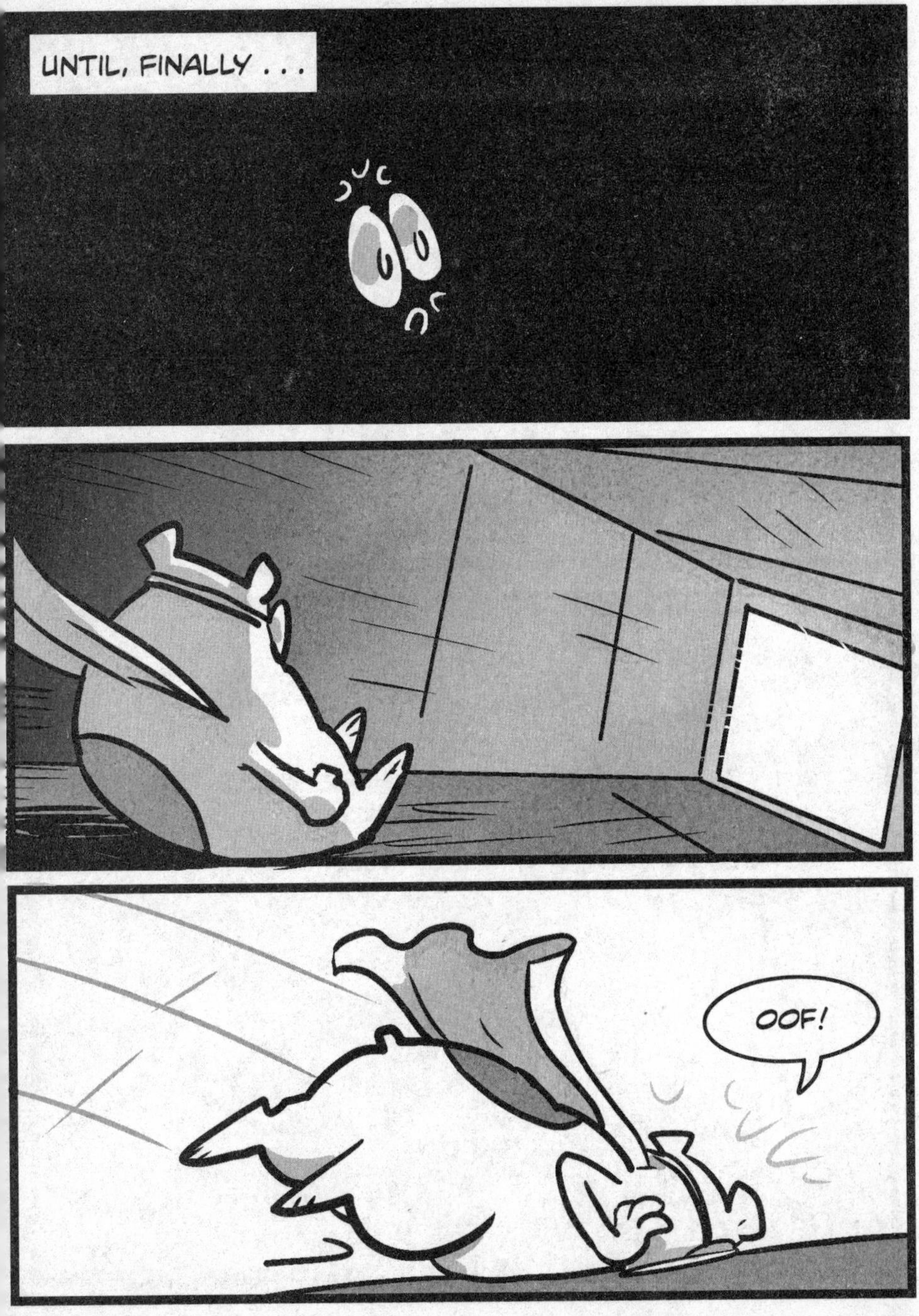
UNTIL, FINALLY . . .
OOF!

Through the vent, Super Turbo could just make out what seemed to be a light switch in the boiler room. "It's too far!" he said, reaching.

"Wait!" said Captain Chameleon. "I think I can turn it on with my tongue!"

"With your tongue?" asked Super Turbo.

Captain Chameleon opened her mouth, and suddenly a superlong tongue shot out.

"Wow!" said Super Turbo. "Nice work, Captain!"

With the lights now on, the super-pets could get a sense of what was on the other side of the vent. Wonder Pig used her super-pig strength to carefully open the vent cover.

Once it was open, it was clear that the boiler room was a place they wanted to get in and out of as quickly as possible. Spooky shadows danced along the walls. There were tons of crazy pipes and vents. The air seemed heavy and warm. In the middle of the room was the boiler itself, giving off a strange hum.

"Hey, Super Turbo, remember when we thought that pencil sharpener in your classroom was scary?" whispered Wonder Pig.

Super Turbo nodded.

"Well, this is way, way scarier," she said.

Super Turbo had to agree. "We'd better figure out how to turn off the water—and fast," he said. "Professor Turtle said there are controls for the heat, the air-conditioning, and the water. We have to find the right one!"

"I'll scout it out!" said the Green Winger, taking off.

Soon she landed on a pipe on the other side of the room. "Well, this one has a label that says 'water,' so I'm guessing this could be it," she announced.

THERE'S A KNOB WE NEED TO TURN! OOF! I CAN'T BUDGE IT!

"Well, it's a good thing we have Wonder Pig's super-pig strength on our side!" cried Super Turbo.

"Not me, Super Turbo," said Wonder Pig. "Look where that pipe is! Green Winger will have to fly one of us to the knob, and it's going to have to be you."

The Green Winger, Captain Chameleon, and Wonder Pig all looked at Super Turbo.

It was suddenly clear to Super Turbo that the fate of this school lay in his paws.

"He did it!" yelled Wonder Pig. "Did he do it?"

The Green Winger cocked her head to one side to listen. "That weird hum has stopped! I think that was the sound of the water rushing!"

"He *did* do it!" cried Wonder Pig, pumping her fist in the air.

"I did do it," Super Turbo said, smiling to himself.

ONE LAST MISSION

Meanwhile, upstairs, the Great Gecko, Boss Bunny, Fantastic Fish, and Professor Turtle were doing all they could to stop the flood from the water fountain. They had made a pretty good dam out of sponges and chalkboard erasers when Professor Turtle noticed something.

"Hey," he said. "I think . . . the water has . . . stopped!"

The Great Gecko looked up from what he was doing. "It has?"

"It sure has!" answered a voice from above.

SUPER TURBO!

"I knew you guys would do it!" said the Great Gecko, patting Super Turbo on the back.

"We all did it," Super Turbo corrected him. "You guys did a great job cleaning up what you could."

"The rest . . . of the water . . . will evaporate . . . ," said Professor Turtle.

"It's been a long night, superpets," said the Great Gecko. "And now I say we all turn in. Unless . . ."

Super Turbo couldn't imagine what the Great Gecko could possibly want to do besides go to sleep.

"Unless you guys want to come with me to grab some snacks from the cafeteria," the Great Gecko finished, smiling.

"After all, half the fun of being a superpet is doing things the schoolkids and teachers will never know about!" Super Turbo said with a grin. "Let's just not turn any knobs or flick any switches this time," he added.

HOORAY FOR THE SUPERPET SUPERHERO LEAGUE!